The KNIGHT and the DRAGON

STORY AND PICTURES BY
TOMIE DEPAOLA

PAPERSTAR

The Putnam & Grosset Group

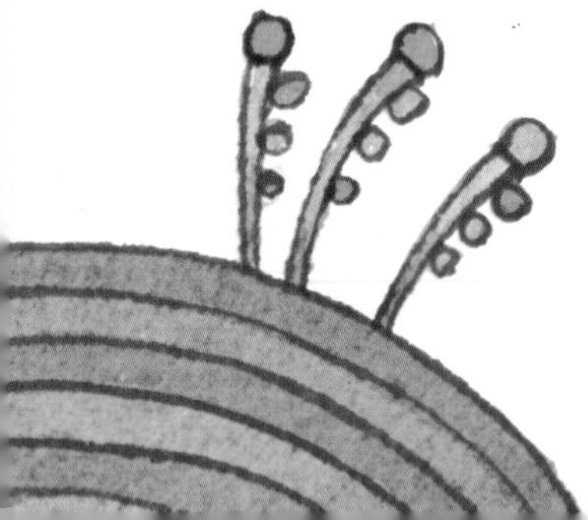

For all my friends in Red Wing

A PaperStar Book, published in 1998 by The Putnam & Grosset Group,
345 Hudson Street, New York, NY 10014.
PaperStar Books is a registered trademark of The Putnam Berkley Group, Inc.
The PaperStar logo is a trademark of The Putnam Berkley Group, Inc.
Originally published in 1980 by G. P. Putnamís Sons.
Published simultaneously in Canada.
Manufactured in China
Library of Congress Cataloging-in-Publication Data
dePaola, Tomie The knight and the dragon
Summary: A knight who has never fought a dragon and an equally
inexperienced dragon prepare to meet each other in battle.
[1. Knights and knighthood—Fiction. 2. Dragons—Fiction.]
I. Title PZ7.D439Kn [E] 79-18131
ISBN 978-0-698-11623-8
22 23 24 25 26 27 28 29 30

Once upon a time, there was a knight in a castle who had never fought a dragon.

And in a cave not too far away was a dragon who had never fought a knight.

One day the knight went to the castle library and took out all of the books he could find on dragon fighting.

Meanwhile, back at the cave, the dragon had rummaged through all the things from his ancestors and found some books on knight fighting.

The knight began to build some armor.

The dragon practiced swishing his tail.

Meanwhile, back at the castle...

Meanwhile, back at the cave...

Finally, the knight and the dragon were both ready.
They sent each other a letter and set a time for…

the fight.

THE OUTDOOR COOK BOOK
HOW TO BUILD A BAR-B-Q

THE OUTDOOR COOK BOOK
HOW TO BUILD A BAR-B-Q

K&D

K & D
B. DRAGON - SIR KNIGHT, PROPS.
BAR-B-Q